ELLI
The LITTLE PENNSYLVANIA ELK

Written and Illustrated by MARK WEAVER

© 2009 Mark Weaver
ISBN: 978-1-884687-84-6
Library of Congress Control Number: 2001012345
All rights reserved. No portion of this book may be reproduced in any manner (photocopying, electronically, or otherwise) without the express written permission of the author.
4th Printing 2021
Printed in the U.S.A.
Comprehensive Printing Solutions
2142 High Hill Road
Pulaski, PA 16143
724-944-8290

It was a crisp sunny morning in early June when Elli entered her wild green world in north central Pennsylvania. Elli was a baby girl elk. She weighed about thirty pounds. Her soft coat was reddish brown with faint white spots. Mother Elk thought her new baby was beautiful.

Just minutes after she was born, Elli was able to take a few unsteady steps on her long wobbly legs. Her lovely light brown mother stood patiently as Elli pushed and butted to get the warm nutritious milk.

During her first month Elli spent most of her time drinking Mother's milk and sleeping. While Mother was grazing, Elli would lay hidden among the cool ferns or in the tall grass. One day a mean looking animal came near the hiding place. Suddenly Mother appeared and chased the hungry coyote far from little Elli.

When about a month old, Elli began nibbling at the tender leaves and grasses around her. Mother did not allow her to drink milk as often as before. They soon joined a small herd. Elli was so excited when she met other calves! Wapi, a little boy elk, became her best friend.

Elli and Wapi and their friends spent their days running and jumping and playing tag and follow-the-leader. They loved to splash in the water. Sometimes squirrels sat on low branches and scolded them for being too noisy.

Elli and her friends shared their world with many other forest creatures. A mother fox and her cubs lived in a den among the rocks. Sometimes Elli watched a family of skunks – from a distance!

White-tailed deer often fed near Elli's herd. The deer looked much like elk, but were not nearly as big. Once Elli saw Mama Raccoon teaching her youngsters how to catch crayfish in the creek.

When they saw a black bear and her cubs across a stream, Elli and Wapi quickly ran back to their mothers.

Timber rattlers lived in rocky outcroppings on the hillsides. If Elli heard a warning rattle, she quickly turned away from the angry snake.

A few months earlier the antlers had fallen from the heads of the bulls. The ones now growing were covered with a fuzzy "velvet". The bulls had to be very careful because their new soft antlers could be easily injured.

In late summer Elli saw bulls rubbing small trees to remove the velvet from their antlers. These damaged trees are called "bull rubs" or "elk rubs".

Often now the bulls lifted their heads and bugled their loud challenges into the brisk air. The sounds of their clashing antlers could be heard in the fields and forests. They were fiercely fighting for the right to mate with the cows.

Elli was scared when a big bull began "bullying" her mother and the other cows. He was now master of the harem and every elk in the herd had to do as he directed.

The days grew cooler. Greens turned to red and gold. Turkeys talked to each other as they scratched to find acorns hidden under the colorful carpet of leaves.

And then something exciting happened! Cold white flakes floated from the gray November sky. They tickled Elli's eyelashes and tingled her nose.

Elli and her friends loved to play in their new white world.

But it was not fun when the snow piled deeper and deeper. Then a freezing rain made a shell of ice on top of the snow.

Now it was hard to walk.

And it was harder to run!

It was not easy to break the crust and scrape the snow from the frozen grass. It was not easy to stretch high to reach the tender twigs. Elli and her friends were often tired and hungry. Winter was long and cold.

At last Elli felt a trace of warmth in the March air. The snow began to melt. Birds returned from their winter vacations. Tender grasses poked their bright green heads through the soil. Elli and the other yearlings sensed new life all around them. Their eyes brightened. Once again they felt like running and jumping and playing their elk calf games.

But this was also a sad time for Elli. Her mother would soon have a new baby calf. Elli could no longer stay with her. Elli wondered if she could ever be happy again.

Then Elli looked around. She saw all her yearling friends. And there was her very best friend Wapi - he looked so cute with those bumps on his head! And they all still lived together in this beautiful wild green world in Pennsylvania. Elli felt better already.

North central Pennsylvania is a beautiful area of hills and low mountains covered with streams, forests, and fields. For thousands of years Native Americans lived here in harmony with the wapiti (pale deer), killing them for food and hides only when necessary. Then the early pioneers pushed westward and as the human population increased, the number of Eastern Elk decreased, until the last one was killed around 1867. Rocky Mountain Elk were brought to Pennsylvania beginning in 1913 but because of hunting, poaching, crop damage control, road kill, and disease, only about 30 animals remained in 1974. Over the next decades, cooperation between the Pennsylvania Game Commission, The Department of Conservation and Natural Resources, and The Rocky Mountain Elk Foundation has resulted in today's healthy elk herd.

Coyotes eat mostly mice, rabbits, and birds. They usually mate for life and live in a den where 6 or 7 pups are born each spring.

Eastern bluebirds eat berries and insects. They usually nest in holes in trees or in special nesting boxes. During autumn they migrate south from the northeastern states.

Elk or wapiti live in forests and open land and feed on grasses and tree browse. Large bulls weigh over one thousand pounds. Each mother usually has one calf in the spring.

Gray squirrels live in hollow trees or in nests of leaves in the branches. They eat seeds, acorns, and nuts which they also store for the winter months.

Northern cardinals feed on open ground looking for insects, fruit and seeds. Some remain in the north over winter.

Raccoons eat almost anything. They live in dens, often in hollow trees, where they sleep during the coldest days of winter.

Crows are omnivorous, which means they eat almost anything, animal or vegetable. They are very intelligent.

Robins are common across America. They migrate in the fall. They eat fruit, insects, and earthworms.

Black bears are omnivorous and they can weigh several hundred pounds. They sleep most of the winter in a den.

Black-capped chickadees are constantly active searching for insects, seeds and berries. They live in or near wooded areas and do not migrate.

Blue jays usually eat nuts, seeds, fruit, and insects. They do not sing but they noisily squawk and often mimic the cries of other birds. Some stay in the north over the winter.

Cottontail rabbits live in underground burrows and produce many babies each year. They eat grasses and other green plants.

Red foxes live in dens in the rocks or on the ground. They eat field mice, rabbits, birds, decaying meat and fruit.

Skunks stink! They live in underground burrows and are omnivorous.

Timber rattlesnakes usually live in rocky dens. They eat small animals and birds and hibernate during the winter. They are poisonous! Their rattle means, "Stay Away!".

White-tailed deer live in forests and farmlands and eat mostly leaves and grasses. The doe usually has two fawns each spring.

Wild turkeys eat insects, berries, seeds, acorns, and nuts. They roost high in the trees at night.

Canada geese are probably the most familiar waterfowl in North America. They eat mainly grasses and other vegetation and are often seen flying in a V-formation.

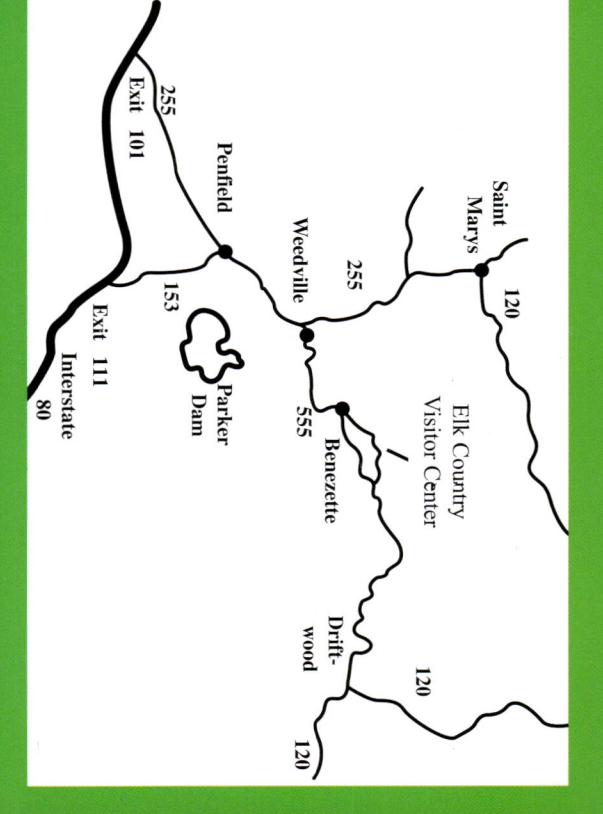

You may be one of the fifty million people who live within six hours of the largest herd of free-roaming elk in Northeastern United States. Why not take a road trip through the beautiful Penn's Woods to Benezette, Pennsylvania? Just one-half hour off Interstate 80 and you're in elk country!

But there are more than elk to see. The ELK COUNTRY VISITOR CENTER is open to the public. Here you can enjoy interactive exhibits and learn about local wildlife. In the 4D Theater you will appreciate the story of Pennsylvania elk. Be sure to browse the gift shop and walk the short nature trails. Elk Country is a great place to visit!